To Liam – DK
For Dr Charmz – GP

First published in 2011 by Scholastic Children's Books
Euston House, 24 Eversholt Street
London NW1 1DB
a division of Scholastic Ltd
www.scholastic.co.uk
London ~ New York ~ Toronto ~ Sydney ~ Auckland
Mexico City ~ New Delhi ~ Hong Kong

Text copyright © 2011 Diana Kimpton
Illustrations copyright © 2011 Garry Parsons

PB ISBN 978 1407 110 87 5

DOCTOR HOOF

Diana Kimpton & Garry Parsons

SCHOLASTIC

When **Doctor Hoof** moved to town,
he nailed a notice to his new front door.

Then he sat back and waited for his patients to arrive.

He waited and waited.

But nobody came.
This was a one-horse town and that one horse was **Doctor Hoof.**

By the end of the week, **Doctor Hoof** felt very lonely.

"This isn't the right place for me," he decided. "I'd better move somewhere else."

He was just starting to pack, when there was a knock at the door.

"I'm Basil Bray,"
whispered the donkey.
"And my throat is very sore."

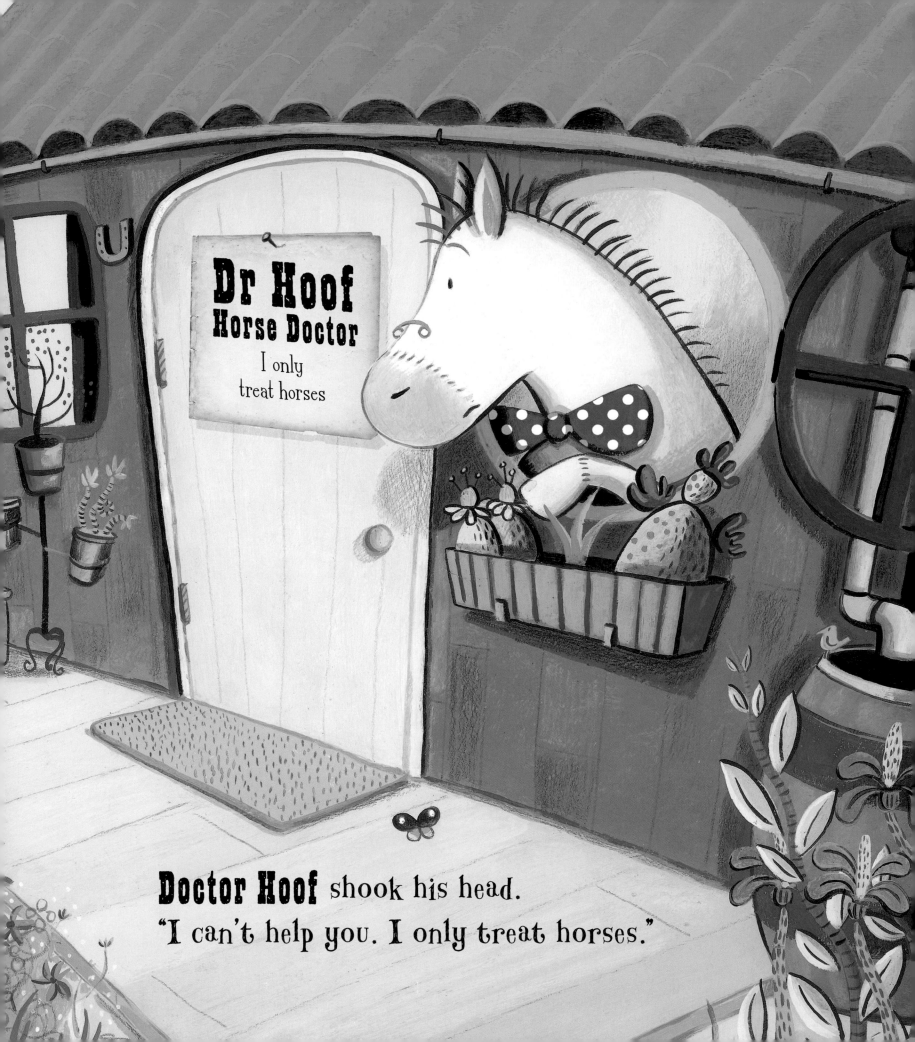

Dr Hoof
Horse Doctor
I only
treat horses

Doctor Hoof shook his head.
"I can't help you. I only treat horses."

"But donkeys aren't very different," said Basil. "Look! I've got hooves, just like you."

Doctor Hoof realised Basil was right. So he gave him some medicine to make him feel better.

Helping Basil made **Doctor Hoof** feel better too!

So he changed the notice on his front door.

Dr Hoof Horse Doctor
I only treat horses
and donkeys

A little while later, there was another knock on the door.
"I'm Walter Woof," said the dog. "I've got a thorn in my foot."

Dr Hoof
Horse Doctor
I only
treat horses
and donkeys

Doctor Hoof shook his head.
"I can't help you. I only
treat horses and donkeys."

"But dogs aren't very different," said Walter. "Look! I've got four legs and a tail, just like you."

Doctor Hoof realised Walter was right. So he pulled the thorn out of the dog's paw to make him feel better.

Helping Walter made Doctor Hoof feel better too!

Dr Hoof
Horse Doctor
I only
treat horses
and donkeys
and dogs

Doctor Hoof went inside again. Almost
immediately, there was another knock on the door.

"I'm Henrietta Hop,"
said the mother rabbit.
"My son, Harry, has cut his ear."

Doctor Hoof shook his head.

"I'm a horse doctor. I only treat
horses and donkeys and dogs.
But I'm sure you're going to tell me
that rabbits aren't very different . . ."

"Of course I'm not," said Mrs Hop. "Rabbits aren't like horses at all!"

"My ear hurts," said Harry, and he started to cry.

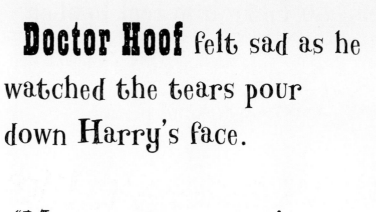

Doctor Hoof felt sad as he watched the tears pour down Harry's face.

"Maybe rabbits aren't very different to horses. My ear would hurt too if I cut it."

He put some ointment and a bandage
on Harry's ear to make him feel better.

Mrs Hop gave Harry a carrot for being brave,
and she gave **Dr Hoof** a carrot for being kind.

Helping Harry had made **Doctor Hoof** feel much better!

He went to the front door and changed his sign again.

Dr Hoof
Horse Doctor

I only treat horses

and donkeys

and dogs

and rabbits

Doctor Hoof crunched his carrot thoughtfully as he read the new sign.

Then he had
a better idea.

He picked up his pencil again and changed
his sign one last time.

From then on, **Doctor Hoof**
had lots of patients . . .

...and lots of friends!

And he never thought of moving again.

The End